Puffin Books

THE COMIC STRIP ODYSSEY

When Odysseus the mighty Greek warrior defeats the Trojans he thinks his troubles are over. But he hasn't reckoned with the Gods. Poseidon the sea god is furious with Odysseus for destroying Troy and he sets out to cause TROUBLE. He churns up the sea and forces Odysseus and his crew to deal with monsters, witches and beautiful goddesses. However, Athene, goddess of wisdom, protects Odysseus, and after twenty years he finally reaches his home. But his house is full of strangers, all wanting to marry Penelope his wife, and his son Telemachus doesn't recognize him. Odysseus sets up a task that only he will be able to carry out, so ending this classic story from Ancient Greece.

A unique retelling of Homer's tale.

Diane Redmond is a versatile writer of books and plays for children. She lives in Cambridge with her family. Robin Kingsland is an actor, illustrator and author. He lives in London with his wife Fiona and their cat.

THE COMIC STRIP

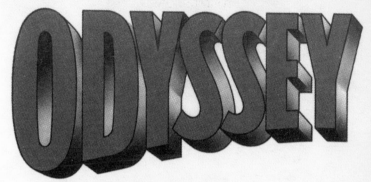

ODYSSEY

Homer's classic,
retold in words and pictures by

DIANE REDMOND
and
ROBIN KINGSLAND

PUFFIN BOOKS

To our friends at the Polka, with love

PUFFIN BOOKS

Published by the Penguin Group
Penguin Books Ltd, 27 Wrights Lane, London W8 5TZ, England
Penguin Books USA Inc., 375 Hudson Street, New York, New York 10014, USA
Penguin Books Australia Ltd, Ringwood, Victoria, Australia
Penguin Books Canada Ltd, 10 Alcorn Avenue, Toronto, Ontario, Canada M4V 3B2
Penguin Books (NZ) Ltd, 182–190 Wairau Road, Auckland 10, New Zealand

Penguin Books Ltd, Registered Offices: Harmondsworth, Middlesex, England

First published by Viking 1992
Published in Puffin Books 1993
1 3 5 7 9 10 8 6 4 2

Based on the play written by Diane Redmond, first performed at the Polka
Children's Theatre, Wimbledon, London, in 1990

Text copyright © Diane Redmond, 1992
Illustrations copyright © Robin Kingsland, 1992
All rights reserved

The moral right of the author has been asserted

Printed in England by Clays Ltd, St Ives plc
Set in Helvetica

WHO'S WHO IN THE COMIC STRIP ODYSSEY

GREEKS

Odysseus, King of Ithaca
Penelope, his wife
Telemachus, their son
Eurylochus) Officers in
Polites) Odysseus' army

GODS

Zeus, greatest of the gods
Hermes, messenger of the gods
Poseidon, the sea god
Athene, goddess of wisdom
Calypso, a lesser goddess
Circe, a witch and a lesser goddess

MONSTERS

Polyphemus, the Cyclops
The Sirens
The Lotus Eaters
Scylla, the six-headed monster
Charybdis, the whirlpool

OTHERS

Alcinous, King of the Phaeacians
Aeolus, King of Aeolia
Eumaeus, a swineherd and loyal servant of Odysseus
The Suitors
Argos, Odysseus' dog
The Soul of Tiresias, a blind prophet

JUST A FREAK MIST, EURYLOCHUS. IT'LL SOON PASS OVER.
OOOO, I DON'T LIKE THIS A BIT, POLITES.
THERE, YOU SEE? IT'S GONE!
ER...
I HATE TO WORRY YOU, POLITES, BUT.....

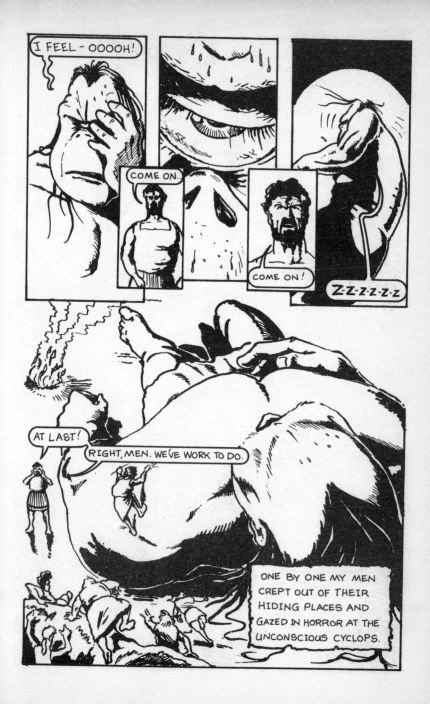

AAAARR

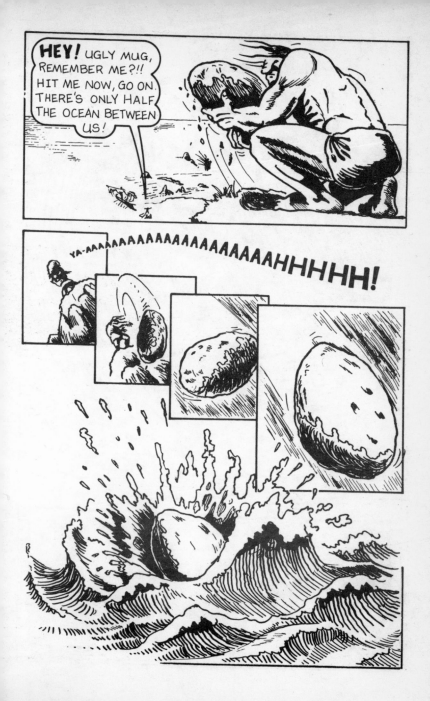

TATTERED AND TORN, WE STEERED OUR BLASTED SHIP ACROSS THE WINE-DARK SEAS —

AND CAME AT LAST TO THE LAND OF KING AEOLUS.

OF COURSE! BUT HOW CAN I FIGHT A GOD?
THE GODDESS ATHENE PROTECTS YOU, MORTAL. YOU SAW HER POWER OVER ME. PERHAPS SHE CAN OUTWIT THE SEA GOD.
I NEED ADVICE. WHO CAN GUIDE ME OUT OF THIS MESS?
TIRESIAS.
I'LL GO TO HIM RIGHT NOW.
NOT SO HASTY, GREEK. TIRESIAS LIVES IN HADES, IN THE VALLEY OF THE SHADOWS. DO YOU HAVE THE COURAGE TO TRAVEL TO HELL AND BACK?
DO I REALLY HAVE ANY CHOICE?
HAVE YOUR CREW AND YOUR SHIP READY AT DAWN. I WILL GUIDE YOU TO HELL AND YOUR CUNNING WILL BRING YOU BACK!

LEAVING SCYLLA AND CHARYBDIS FAR BEHIND.

FOR DAYS WE DRIFTED, BATTLE-WORN AND STARVING. THEN WE CAME TO AN ISLAND WHERE CATTLE GRAZED IN ROLLING MEADOWS.

NOTHING ON EARTH CAN SAVE YOUR MEN, ODYSSEUS. THEY WILL DIE. BUT YOU CAN LIVE, IF YOU LEAVE NOW. SWIM, RUN, WALK ON WATER - JUST GET AWAY, **NOW!**